There's only a window between us now. I break through it.

"You...you're...you're...*dead!*" the Professor stutters.

I grab him tightly. "Am I...dead?" I say. "Is...that what...you've...done to me?...Made me a walking...*dead man?*"

"You're an animal," the Professor spits out. "A trained animal."

"*I...am...Logan!*" I say. "I...am...a man. You...are the...animal!"

Wolverine: Top Secret

by Francine Hughes

cover illustration by Dana and Del Thompson

text illustrations by Aristides Ruiz

Bullseye Books

Random House New York

A BULLSEYE BOOK PUBLISHED BY RANDOM HOUSE, INC.

Library of Congress Catalog Card Number: 93-73459
ISBN: 0-679-86004-5
RL: 2.5

Manufactured in the United States of America   10 9 8 7 6 5 4 3 2 1

X-MEN

Wolverine:
Top Secret

The Present: The X-Men's Mansion Westchester County, New York

Music. Lightning. Punches flying. Wolves. Pictures coming and going. Guns. Helicopters. Claws. Scenes shifting like a kaleidoscope. Around and around. Growing dizzy...

I wake up. My heart is pounding. I'm sweating like a pig.

"Calm down, bub," I say to myself. "You're just dreamin'." Again.

I have these dreams—nightmares, really— all the time. Night and day. Flashes of memories that make no sense to me. Some of them are good, but mostly they're bad. Real bad. When it happens around the X-Men, I act like it doesn't bother me. But deep down I don't feel so good. I feel sick. Lost.

I lie back on my pillow, trying to forget. I'm safe in my bed in the X-Men's mansion. Music. Lightning. Wolves. All those pictures! They've been bouncing around my head for as long as I can remember. Guns. Helicopters. Fights I was never in! They seem so real.

Are they?

Who knows? I don't know anything about my past. Not where I grew up. Or who my parents were. If I even had parents.

It ain't easy being me.

Sure, I can hunt down any animal, any man. My claws can rip apart a tiger like a cotton ball. My skeleton's bonded with adamantium—supposedly the strongest metal known to man. And if an opponent is lucky enough to injure me, my accelerated mutant healing factor allows my body to heal fast—frighteningly fast.

But it's not my claws or my healing factor that makes me a walking, talking weapon. It's me. Something deep inside. I'm bad to the bone...the adamantium-laced bone. That's the problem. Where does *that* come from? Who am I?

What am I?

I walk over to the mirror and stare at my face. Light from the floodlit basketball court behind the mansion filters into my room. The X-Men are playing a night game. They asked me to join them. I declined. Need my beauty rest.

"Okay, bub," I say. "Let's solve this mystery. Let's think."

The X-Men's shouts drift up to my window. But I block out the noise. I've got to concentrate.

Get my mind focused.

All right. My name is Logan. Sometimes I see certain scenes, certain places. Flashbacks. Memories. I think they're real. But the memory always fades. And it's replaced by another one, before I can understand it.

Tonight when I dream, I'm going to *remember*. I am going to make some *sense* of my life. I sit on the bed, head in hands.

"Logan...Logan..." That voice. It belongs to a girl named Silver Fox. Please let *her* be real.

Slowly, it all comes back...

CHAPTER 1

The Prom

Lockers. Hallways. Classrooms. A poster for a homecoming parade. I'm in high school. And late for gym.

I hurry down the hall. Kids give me plenty of room. They're afraid of me. I feel different from them. And I sure look different in my old flannel shirt, faded jeans, and army boots. Where are these kids going, anyway? They look like they're dressed for a tea party.

I'm not exactly Mr. Popularity here. I spend a lot of time working on my motorcycle. They call me "Greaser."

A group of guys stop and stare at me, and I

give them a dirty look. Let them be afraid! What a bunch of punks. I'm not very tall. Only five foot eight. But I'm solid. And strong as a...as a I don't know what!

Still the guys stare. They're challenging me. Idiots. I can't be bothered fighting them. Girls, on the other hand, look through me like I'm not even here. So I keep quiet. I don't care about having friends. At least that's what I tell myself.

We're running laps around the track in gym when the coach calls me over. I've passed everyone else three times already.

"Hey, Logan," he says, motioning me to stop. "Why don't you try out for football this year? You're the best athlete we've got. Best anyone's got."

"Thanks, but no thanks," I tell him.

Me? On a team? I don't even *attend* sporting events—no football games or pep rallies, not any school stuff. I can barely make myself go to class.

I start to run again. I like being on the move, using my muscles. I know I'm strong.

And quick, too. Amazingly quick. And then there's this other special thing about me. Something that's, well...really *strange*. It frightens me a bit. When I injure my body, it heals inhumanly fast.

I don't let anyone know about that.

Suddenly, somebody sticks his foot in my way. I go down—*smack*—face first into the ground.

The coach rushes over. "I think you've broken your nose, son."

He tries to help me up, but I brush him off. "I'm okay," I say. "Really." I don't want him to see what's happening. Already my nose is healing. It only takes a second. It's like it was never even broken.

The coach gives me a strange look. "Well," he says. "I thought it was broken." He backs off. All the kids do. I turn away. More than anything, I want to be alone.

I don't need any friends. I don't need anybody.

After school, I take my bike for a spin. With the wind in my face, I forget everything and everybody. Here in the Canadian mountains, you can ride for miles and not see a single person.

I decide to head for the Indian reservation. I've never been there, but I've heard people talk about it. They say the Indians are no good. That they're less than human. Sounds like I feel, sometimes.

At the reservation, I get off my bike and look around. The place looks abandoned. Just a few burned-out shacks in a clearing in the woods. One brick building still stands. No people around.

I'm back on my bike, ready to take off, when I catch sight of someone. A girl.

She's darting from tree to tree, watching me. She's quick. But so am I. She knows I've seen her. In a flash, she disappears into the woods.

I start to go after her, but change my mind. "So what?" I tell myself. "She's just another girl."

Besides, I've got to get home. I have to make dinner for the old man.

I arrive. And the old man's in a bad mood. He's been talking to the coach.

"What's with you, boy?" he says. "Why don't you try out for the team? What else are you so busy doing? Where were you after school today?"

I don't know why he's bothering. All he wants is dinner. Not conversation. He's never cared where I go or what I do.

So I tell the truth. "I went to the Indian reservation today."

"The reservation!" he says. "You stay away from that kind, boy. You have enough trouble. You got to go look for more?"

He storms from the table, knocking over his soup. I stay calm. I pick up the bowl and clean up the mess. I hadn't planned on going back to the reservation. Except for the girl, it seemed pretty dull. But if it bothers him so much...

I skip school the next day and head back. I wonder if I'll see the girl again. I do.

She's sitting on the steps of the brick building. Her long arms are wrapped around her knees, and her face is tilted toward the sun. Her eyes are closed. I sneak closer to her. She's very pretty. Much prettier than any girl I've ever seen. Her hair falls in a long braid down her back.

She's so still, it's like she's part of the scenery. I'm so close I can almost touch her.

Suddenly, she whips out her arm and grabs my ankle. The next thing I know I'm flat on my back. Her foot is pressing against my neck.

"Who are you?" she asks. "And what are you doing here? You want to look at the damage? See how my village was destroyed? Burned down by white teenagers for a joke!"

"My name is Logan," I choke out. "And I'm here to...well, to see *you*. And I don't think there's anything funny about what was done to your home."

She lets go of me. We both sit on the steps.

"My name is Silver Fox," she says, looking me in the eye with a small smile. I know she's different. Not because she's an Indian. But because she's quick. Powerful. As powerful as me. She's different the same way I'm different.

Every day after school I go up to the reservation. Silver Fox and I track animals through the woods. No matter what the weather is, we run and hike and swim. We laugh a lot, too.

I can't believe I have a friend. A friend who's a beautiful girl.

Then one day, some guys from school follow me in a car to the reservation. I know they're there. But I'm too happy to care.

Silver Fox and I are sitting under a tree, talking, when the guys approach.

"Stick with your own kind, Logan," one named Ted says. "Even you can do better than some dirty squaw!"

Silver Fox draws in her breath. The next thing I know, she's gone.

I tell them to get lost, and then I take off after Silver Fox. I search everywhere, but can't find her.

The next day at school, the kids won't leave me alone. "Hey, Chief Likes-Squaws-a-Lot," they call out from every corner. "Yo, Indian Greaser!" When I pass them in the halls, they make Indian war cries. They even stuff feathers in my locker.

I'm angry, but what can I do? Fight the entire school? The only thing that keeps me going is Silver Fox.

I go back to the reservation that afternoon. Silver Fox is building a fire. "Hello, Logan," she says quietly. "I wasn't sure you'd be back."

"I'd never leave you, Silver Fox," I say. I hold her close and kiss her. "Those guys are idiots. We have to stand up to them. Act like nothing has happened. Come with me to the school prom."

At first Silver Fox says no. But then I tell her about the music, the dancing, the lights. I've never been to a prom. But I've heard about them. And the thought of going with Silver Fox as my date makes the whole thing seem like fun.

"Everything will be fine," I say. "They'll forget about us."

"Okay, Logan," she says. "If you think it will be all right."

Silver Fox said yes!

The next few weeks pass in a blur. I take a

job in the lumberyard after school. I work from 4 P.M. until midnight. It's tough work, but the money is good. And I need the money to rent a tux.

Suddenly it's the night of the prom. Silver Fox is more beautiful than ever.

"You're like an Indian princess," I tell her.

And hey—I don't look too bad myself. The monkey suit is a bit tight, though.

We walk into the high school gym, holding hands. It looks so different. There are balloons and streamers and tables set up with flowers and tablecloths. The band is playing a slow romantic song.

"Hey, little darlin'," I say with a bow. "Would you care to dance?"

Silver Fox laughs and holds out her hand. We dance. People smile at us. A few even wave.

Then the band takes a break. A couple of guys come over. One gives me a friendly punch in the shoulder. It's Ted.

"Hey, Logan," he says. "How you guys doing?"

"Okay," I answer carefully

"I'm glad you could make it. I want to tell you how sorry I am for the way we acted the other week.

"I just got a new motorcycle," he adds, smiling. "Want to take a look at it?"

His date comes over and loops her arm through Silver Fox's. "We'll get some punch," she says.

Silver Fox nods. She must feel the same way I do. Things are turning around.

I follow Ted out to the parking lot. "So where's your..." I start to say when four guys jump me from behind a car.

"You don't get it, do you, greaser?" Ted says. "You just don't know your place. Who do you think you are, bringing one of *them* to *our* prom?"

Two of them hold me while the others punch and kick me. I fall to the ground like a piece of garbage. Then I hear Silver Fox's voice. That sweet, tender voice. "Logan?" she calls.

The goons run away, and Silver Fox rushes over. She kneels down to help me.

"That girl told me what they were doing,"

she says. "Oh, Logan!"

Suddenly, everything is just too much. First I fall for Ted's trick. And now Silver Fox is seeing me like this! I'm broken...defeated... and mad. Too mad to think straight.

Too mad to remember what happened next.

So mad that I wake up, back in the X-Men's mansion. What happened next? Did I run from Silver Fox? Or did I let her help me? I don't have a clue.

I shake my head to clear it. For a second, I'm back in the high school parking lot. But then the parking lot disappears. Instead, I see...

CHAPTER 2

....

The Cabin

Bright stars. Full moon. Tall trees. I'm in the Canadian mountains, chopping wood.

There's a cabin in the distance. Our cabin—mine and Silver Fox's. It's a cold, clear night. You'd never know it was spring. Except for the sound of my ax hitting wood, it's quiet as a church.

But then I hear something whimper. I squint in the moonlight and see a shape lying under a pine tree. An animal? I hear the whimper again, and move a little closer. It's a dog.

I know that dog. Silver Fox and I first saw him about a month ago. He was running through the woods. We even said, "What a handsome dog." Graceful. We tried to get close to him, but he wouldn't let us. He ran away. But we got a good look. No dog tag. No collar.

A wild dog. A beautiful wild dog. He licks and chews at his paw. He's hurt. As quietly as I can, I move closer.

"Hey, boy," I say in a low, soothing voice. "It's okay. I want to help you. That's all. Just help you."

Slowly I inch forward. The dog flinches. But he doesn't move away. I reach out my hand and crouch down next to him.

For a while I just hold out my hand, which he sniffs. He seems to relax, and I touch his paw. He whimpers more, but lets me examine it. There's a big pine needle stuck deep in one of his pads.

"Atta boy," I say. "This won't hurt, well, almost at all."

I take hold of the pine needle and pull. Fast.

The dog softly wags his tail. He's weak. Probably starving. I gather him in my arms.

"I'm takin' you home, boy," I say, "for some tender loving care."

I carry the dog to the cabin, kick open the door, and bring him inside.

"Logan?" calls Silver Fox from the kitchen.

I set the dog down on the rug in front of the fire and go into the kitchen. Silver Fox is putting away the dinner dishes. She smiles when she sees me and pours out a steaming mug of coffee.

"I thought you'd need some warming up," she says, handing me the cup.

I put down the coffee and wrap her in my arms. "Darlin'," I tell her, "the best kind of warming I know doesn't take cream and sugar." I kiss her.

"You were gone a long time," she says when I step away. "Did you chop down the whole forest?"

"Not exactly," I say with a smile.

"Well, what have you been doing?"

"Oh, I've been busy." I can't resist teasing her. "I've brought something home for us. Something we never thought we could have."

"You've bought something? Logan, you know we can't afford anything."

It's true. Our bank account ain't exactly bursting with money. In fact, we don't even have a bank account! Just a few bucks stashed in our mattress. But we get by. We live off the land, hunting and fishing. And Silver Fox is an expert forager. She knows all the edible plants that grow wild in the forest. We even grow a garden in the summer.

I'm lucky to have Silver Fox. She's smart, funny, beautiful, and can catch a spawning salmon with her bare hands! Maybe I shouldn't push this teasing business. Besides, I don't want to leave the dog alone.

"My surprise didn't cost a cent. Come, let me show you," I say, holding the door open. "After you."

Silver Fox laughs and steps into the other room. She sees the dog and a smile washes over her face. "It's the wild dog!" she says. She rushes over to him and the smile fades. "He's hurt."

She grabs the first aid kit and starts to

work. A few minutes later, the dog has a gauze bandage wrapped around about half his leg. I give her a funny look.

"It's for support, Logan," she explains.

She scratches the dog behind the ears and covers him with kisses. He's a scary-looking beast. Could be part wolf. But Silver Fox isn't afraid. She plays with him like a puppy, and he licks her face. His fur is so dark, it almost looks blue.

"Let's call him Blue," Silver Fox says, like she's read my mind. She hugs the dog tight. "You rest now, little one. We'll take care of you."

A few minutes later, the dog is fast asleep in front of the fire. Silver Fox sits close by him, rocking back and forth in the rocking chair. It's like we're a real family. First one I've ever really had. I laugh out loud when it occurs to me that we *are* one. A family. Still, something inside me says this won't last. Nothing good ever does for me.

I'd like for this to be different. Silver Fox and me and lots of dogs living here forever. No

people to deal with. No problems.

And for a while, we *are* happy. Blue is a great dog. We go hunting together. Fishing. Walking. The three of us.

My little family.

Spring thaw hits, and it starts getting warm. Sunny, sometimes. And I feel myself melt a little, too. I begin to believe that our happiness might last.

One day, I'm sitting at the foot of an old oak tree near the lake. Silver Fox stands by the shore, throwing sticks into the water for Blue to fetch.

I take an old knife from my belt and start carving the tree trunk. I carve LOGAN + SILVER FOX with a heart around it. Corny, I know.

"Hey, darlin'," I call out. "Come over and eyeball this!"

Silver Fox runs over, examines my handiwork, and gives me a kiss. Then Blue comes charging over. He shakes himself dry, getting us good and wet. I laugh and hug him tightly.

We fish for the rest of the afternoon. After we've caught all we can eat, we head back to the cabin. Blue races ahead of us. I whistle for him to slow down, but he just keeps going.

"Here, boy," I call, clapping my hands together. But he's already deep into the woods.

"Let him go," Silver Fox says, her hand on my arm. "He can run through the woods if he wants. He knows the way back."

Part of me wants to run after him. To protect him. But Silver Fox is right. The dog needs his freedom. Besides, he's probably just running back to the cabin.

But when we get back, Blue isn't there. I tell myself he's probably out chasing squirrels or rolling on some great stinking pile of God knows what, having a fine old time. That he'll be back any minute.

We fry up our fish for dinner. By now the sun's set. It's dark and Blue's still not back. I walk outside, looking around. I give a whistle. Nothing.

"Logan," Silver Fox calls. "Come inside. It's late."

Days pass. Still no Blue. I search the woods over and over. I whistle. Call his name.

Nothing.

I can't help worrying. I love that dog. When I get home from hunting, I'm exhausted but I can't sleep. I can't stop thinking about Blue. Just keep busy, I tell myself. Think about something else.

So I light a fire. That takes about half an hour. It's really too hot for one, but the flames give me some comfort against the darkness outside.

Silver Fox kneels beside me. "Don't worry, Logan," she says. "Blue will be back."

"It's been a week."

"I know. But dogs have to go off by themselves sometimes. Just like people. Sometimes they need to be wild, to..."

"Be quiet," I tell her. I hear scuffling outside. "It's Blue!"

I run to open the door. And there is Blue, standing there, staring at me. For a moment he doesn't move. Doesn't even breathe.

Then he lifts his head and howls. It's a strange sound—filled with pain and I don't know what else. He lunges at me, gnashing his teeth. I leap back just in time. He's foaming at the mouth. I know what the matter is. Madness. "Rabies," I say to Silver Fox. "He must've been bit by a rabid coon!" The dog's inside the cabin now. Backed into the corner, facing us. Growling. Dangerous. Deadly.

Silver Fox grabs a rifle hanging on the wall and aims it at the dog. But her hands shake wildly. "I can't do it, Logan," she says, lowering the barrel. "You have to put him down."

I take the rifle and aim it at Blue. My hands are steady. But I don't pull the trigger.

"Shoot him, Logan. Shoot him," Silver Fox is saying. "It must be done!"

Blue edges closer to us. I can't move. Can't shoot.

Silver Fox grabs the rifle from my hands, and pushes me aside. "Wait!" I cry. She doesn't listen. She pulls the trigger.

There's a blast of light. When he's hit, the dog makes a sound that I know I'll remember for the rest of my life.

Blood is seeping out of him. He whimpers—just like he did when I took the needle from his paw. Then he is quiet. Still.

I fall to the floor and cradle him in my arms. Silver Fox stands above us. "I did what had to be done," she says. And then everything is quiet.

Suddenly I can't bear the sight of her, or to be in the same room with her. I carry Blue outside and bury him in a clearing by the cabin. Through the window I see Silver Fox rocking by the fire. The cabin. It all looks the same. But everything's changed.

Blue's gone.

I'm out of here, too. I feel like being wild. Free. Alone.

I shiver in the warm air and turn up my collar. Then I walk away, leaving the cabin, and Silver Fox, behind.

The woods grow darker and the shadows change shape until suddenly I'm not in the woods anymore. I'm somewhere else entirely.

CHAPTER 3

The Army

High fences. Barracks. Guards with guns. The military.

"Left. Left. Left, right, left."

I'm marching with my unit around an army base. "Left my home to move along," the sergeant calls out. "Sound off!"

The other men barely answer. They're tired and dragging their feet. I can hear them breathing heavily with the strain. But I feel good. I could march like this all day.

Afterward, the sergeant says, "Good work, Logan." Victor Creed is his name. He wears the standard army uniform. But he looks somehow different to me. Kind of wild. Like an animal.

My unit breaks into little groups. One guy comes over to me. "A bunch of us are going to the movies," he says. "Want to come?"

"Nope. I got things to do," I tell him. All this being in a group has gotten to me. I need to be alone.

I'm still not tired. So I go to the gym to work out. Sergeant Creed is there, too.

"I've got plans for you, Logan," he says. "And for me, too. Together, nothing can stop us!"

We're standing in front of a mirror, lifting weights. Our eyes meet in the mirror for a moment. Creed smiles. But his eyes look hard. Then he lowers the barbell. I notice the weight he's using. It's a lot more than mine. This guy is one tough son-of-a-gun.

The next day Creed takes me to an obstacle course. It's just him and me. Good. I don't like teamwork.

"Okay, let's see what you've got," he says.

I take off down the course. Creed times me. "Too slow," he tells me. "Do it again. This time keep your body low. Swing hard over the mud puddle. And jump high on the rope ladder so you get a better start."

I do what he says. "Good!" shouts Creed. "You shaved off sixteen seconds. Now do better!"

And that's how it is. The next day we go to the gym. The day after that we head to the mountains. Every day it's a different workout. I feel like I'm a boxer and Creed is my trainer.

"You're going to be one heavy-duty fighting machine," he tells me.

For weeks Creed teaches me how to maneuver through the woods. How to defend myself. Even how to track animals and hunt them down. I barely see the men in my unit, and never speak to them. But it's okay. It's enough to talk to Creed.

"What's the game plan today?" I say to him one morning. "Lifting weights? Running?"

"We're going to try something new," Creed answers. He leads me to the woods. Then he asks me to remove my jacket, gun, boots, and socks.

"Let's see how you run without all this. I bet you're even quicker."

But if I was in combat, I wouldn't be bare-foot. "What's going on?" I ask.

Creed smiles. "Don't worry," he says. "This is great training for emergencies. It'll toughen you up. Besides, I'll be right behind you, timing you every step of the way."

Fine. I don't really care. The guy seems to know what he's doing. A second later, I'm off.

It's a sunny day, but the woods are dark. I can't see the ground. Not too healthy when you're barefoot, I think. Sharp stones and branches cut my feet. My healing factor can't keep up. I run as fast as I can, but I ain't setting any personal best. I turn around to look for Creed. He's not there.

But *somebody* is. Somebody or something. I can sense it.

I hear a low rumble. It can't be thunder. Sounds more like a growl. Suddenly something slashes across my back. It's a wolf! I'm being attacked!

I reach for my gun, remembering too late that I'm unarmed. How can I ward off a pack of wolves? I can't even run for cover. My feet are cut too badly. Where is Creed?

I face the wolves. I have to fight.

There are three of them, eager for a piece of my hide. I grab one around the neck, but the other two come at me from different sides. When they're not fighting me, they fight each other *for* me, like a prize bone.

Losing a lot of blood. Growing weaker. Ground rising up. Spinning...it's all over...

Gunshots. From far away. Everything is

muffled. My brain is fuzzy. More shots. Wolves fall to the ground next to me. A voice.

"I knew you had it in you, Logan. You're a mutant all right. Healing already. Look at those wounds! Beautiful. Let's get you back to the base, pal."

I'm so tired. I close my eyes for a second, and when I open them again everything is white. White walls, white sheets, white uniforms—I'm in the infirmary. My mouth is as dry as a desert.

Creed is sitting on a chair next to my bed. My lips are practically glued together. I can't speak. He pours me some water. "Here," he says. "Drink this." He sits back down and starts telling me how worried he was about me. Right. I know enough to realize this is an act. He *sent* me into those woods. I was set up. He—and God knows who else—wanted to see what the wolves would do to me. He wanted to see if I was a mutant. Didn't he? I'm having trouble concentrating. My vision is blurring.

A nurse comes in to check my temperature. "Normal," she says, smiling. "You're lucky to be alive, Mr. Logan. Your friend here saved your life. He carried you to the infirmary and hasn't left your side since. I must say, you've had the most remarkable recovery I've ever seen."

The nurse leaves. It's just Creed and me.

"You shouldn't have gone into the woods alone," he tells me. "I told you to wait for me. I had to go back to the barracks to get the stopwatch. But no, you couldn't wait. You had to be tough. Thank goodness I made it back in time. I'll tell you, buddy, I thought you were a goner. I carried you for miles!"

Huh? I'm confused. Did Creed really save my life? I have to think. Concentrate. I have to close my eyes—have to stop seeing Creed's face. That smiling, wild face.

That face. I sit up in bed—my own bed in the mansion. For a moment, I'm back in the present. Then I remember another time, another place. But that face is still there. Creed.

CHAPTER 4

•••••••••••••••••••••••

The Mission

A stark gray room. One bare light bulb. No windows. I'm in a military installation.

"You're bluffing, boy." Creed is sitting across from me. He grins. Only it's more like a sneer. And I'd like to wipe it off his face. Instead, I look at the hand he's dealt me. We're playing cards.

"Sorry, Logan," says another man. North is his name. "I've got to go with Creed on this. He can read you like a book."

I don't bother showing my cards. Creed was right. I fling them across the room. I'm tired of playing. I'm tired of waiting around.

Creed, North, and I are on a special mission for the Canadian government. The assignment? To guard a bag of rocks. You'd think the army would have something better for us to do. We are, after all, their top agents. But no. Why should the government make any more sense than the rest of the world?

Sure, I know these rocks are special. They're going to be made into superpowered missile fuel. But the rocks are in a safe. And the safe is being watched by another team of guards. We're here *as backup!* I'm mad, bored to the point of insanity, and losing my shirt playing cards.

Creed makes a big show of picking up my cards. "Temper, temper," he says, shaking his finger at me.

"Listen, Creed," I say. I'm angry at him—more angry than I should be. "Tell you what.

"You and me. We cut the deck. High card wins. Winner takes all."

North tries to stop us. "Calm yourself, Logan," he says. "You take everything too seriously."

But Creed's already shuffling the cards. "You're mistaken," he says to North. "It's Logan who is about to get *seriously taken*—for all his money!"

He puts the deck on the table. "Who first?"

"Age before beauty," I answer. Creed is older than me. Besides, everyone knows I've got a pretty face.

Creed grunts and cuts the deck. "King!" he says, showing me the card.

My turn. I lift the top card.

Suddenly an alarm goes off. The rocks! It's time for action, not cards.

Still, I'm curious. I turn over the card. A jack.

Creed and North are already on their feet, heading for the door.

"Logan!" yells Creed. But he sees the card. There's that grin again.

We burst into the room where the safe is kept. But it's too late. The guards have been killed. The safe is open. And the rocks are gone.

I strain to listen. Footsteps. They're getting fainter. "Our guy's heading for the roof," I say.

"Okay," says Creed. "We split up. I take the back stairs. North, take the front. Logan, take the fire escape."

"Right," I say as I slip out the window and up the fire escape.

There's a puttering noise coming from the roof. A helicopter! I climb quicker. Just one more floor...

I swing myself onto the roof just as the 'copter takes off. Creed and North are nowhere to be seen.

I make a long jump and grab hold of a helicopter runner with my left hand. For one hairy moment, I swing wildly in the air.

I get my other hand onto the runner and raise myself up until my head is level with the door.

All at once, a boot comes down on my hand. Hard. I hold on tight. Two guys are inside the 'copter. One is flying it. The other is clutching the canvas bag full of rocks. He's the one with his foot on my hand.

Below us is water and an occasional big ship.

This guy lifts his foot and is about to bring it down again when I grab it.

"I'm not crazy about your footwear, bub," I say. "Especially in my face." The helicopter is so noisy, I'm not sure he hears me. But he gets the idea. I push the boot with all my strength.

He goes crashing into the pilot.

The 'copter swerves. I almost lose my grip. But almost doesn't count. With one mighty heave, I pull myself up and inside.

The two men look surprised to see me. Their mouths are hanging wide open. It's close quarters. So close I can see their dental work. I just have to lift my elbow to jab the guy with the rocks. Bingo! A direct hit right on the chin and he's sleeping like a baby.

Now the pilot is reaching for a gun.

"We can't have that," I tell him. "Remember, safety first."

I karate-chop his arm. The gun flies loose. *Crack!* It goes off. So much for safety. The windshield is shattered. And the pilot is slumped over the controls.

"Hey, bub," I shout, slapping his cheek.

"Wake up and fly this thing." My words echo in the quiet. Quiet? The pilot must have cut off the engine!

We're falling fast. I push the pilot aside, grabbing frantically at the controls. Nothing. Out of the corner of my eye I see something move. The canvas bag is open on the floor and the rocks are tumbling out of the helicopter!

Sblam! All around me I see blue. Water. It's rushing in. We're sinking fast!

I pull at the two unconscious bodies as hard as I can, but the pressure is too much. They don't budge. There's nothing I can do. It's time for this rat to desert ship. I crawl out and swim for it.

I push myself up, up, up through the water. Come on, knucklehead, I think to myself. You can do it.

My lungs are about to burst when...*ahh!* I've broken the surface. I breathe deeply and tread water, getting my strength back. Time passes. I float on my back. Finally, I hear sirens. It's the Coast Guard.

An hour later, I'm back at the military

installation. I'm soaking wet. But nobody says anything about changing clothes. Instead, I'm ushered through a maze of hallways.

I pass Creed. "Don't forget!" he shouts at me. "You owe me money!"

Nice homecoming, I think. But then I realize where I'm being taken: to the commanding officer.

Hmm. This job might turn out okay, after all. The CO knows I mean business now. Who got to the roof in time? Me! Not Creed. Not North. And who stopped those rock thieves? Me, again! In fact, I almost got killed! That should mean something. A medal? A commendation, maybe?

A secretary waves me in.

The CO is sitting behind a giant desk. There's not a piece of paper in sight. No pens, no pencils—not a sign of work. What does this guy do anyway?

I find out soon enough. He chews people out.

"I'll get straight to the point," he begins. "*Those rocks were your number one priority!* And you lost them. You screwed up big. From now on, hothead, you follow orders! Understand? Dismissed."

I can't believe this! I think as I make my way back to the barracks. It takes a while for the facts to sink in. But then it all makes a weird kind of sense. Of course I'm in trouble. I'm always in trouble. I'm different. And I always will be. And I don't like people telling me what to do.

I make a decision. From now on, I do things my own way. It's that simple. Too bad for Creed. Too bad for the army. Too bad for everyone but me.

Me. Me. Me. The word pounds in my head like a bouncing ball. And then it fades, and I wake to hear a real ball bouncing. It's the X-Men, still shooting hoops. I get up and close the window.

I have to shut out the noise. I have to concentrate. I have to move back through time...

CHAPTER 5

•••••••••••••••••••••

Weapon X/ Phase 1: The Kidnapping

Thunder. Lightning. Pouring rain. A neon sign blinking through my window. I'm at the Hotel Prophecy—a beat-up old fleabag of a joint.

I've just woken from a strange dream. A nightmare where I'm being held prisoner. A nightmare where my hands are turning into daggers.

On, off. On, off. I can't tear my eyes from the neon sign outside my window. A storm rages outside. But there's a storm inside my head, too. I can't shake that nightmare. What does it mean? But that's not the only thing on my mind. I pace the floor, thinking. I have to figure out where to go, what to do.

I've been kicked out of the army.

I have no family. No friends. Nowhere to go. The army has determined I'm too wild. Too violent. I smash my fists against the window. "Too violent? Right. That's a laugh!"

I've got to get out of that room, so I roam the streets. The rain is coming down in buckets, so except for a few lost souls—like me—the streets are empty.

"Hey, you!" says a guy, stepping out from a back alley. He has a pistol in his hand. "I want your money."

"My *money?*" I say. "That's all? Because I want your soul."

I go at him with everything I've got. A minute later, it's over. I've won.

Shoulders stooped, I head back to the hotel. Yeah, I was looking for a fight. And I found it. But fighting didn't make things better. I feel worse than ever.

"Bub," I tell myself, "you've just hit rock bottom. At least there's nowhere to go but up."

In my room, I make a decision. I'm going to head up north to the Yukon. Hang my hat in a big empty space. All by my lonesome.

I throw my stuff in a suitcase. It doesn't take long. I don't carry much baggage.

My car is parked outside. I toss the suitcase in the back and am just about to get in when I hear footsteps.

"Mr. Logan?" I turn. Three suits are standing in front of me. Detectives, I assume.

"Listen, officers," I say. "What seems to be the..."

But before I can finish, one of them shoots me with a stun gun. They rush me. Everything is happening in slow motion. I'm too dazed to react.

I can't fight all of them. Not in this condition. I sink to the ground. The last thing I see is the neon sign. Prophecy. A prediction of things to come. Nightmares...prison...pain.

CHAPTER 6

....

Weapon X/
Phase 2:
The Experiment

Water. Tubes. Glass. I'm floating in some sort
of tank. An aquarium? Cables holding me in
position. Water reeks of chemicals.

What's happening? Everything is fuzzy.
I'm drugged.

Tubes run into my body. Am I on life
support? I feel little pinches all over. Dozens
and dozens of little pinches. Like metal pins
are being pushed under my skin.

I can hear faint voices, see shadowy figures. They're behind a glass wall, looking at me.

"He *has* to be conscious, Professor," one man is saying. "We must be able to monitor his reactions.

"Please observe," he goes on. "The adamantium is fed into his body through the tubes..."

Aaagh! More pinches—especially in my hands.

"...where it bonds at a cellular level with the bones, making a metal skeleton."

Adamantium? What are they talking about? They mention something called Weapon X. *Weapon X?*

"Look," a woman says. "He was brought here in pretty bad shape. Now he's all healed. This can't be possible. I think there's something very strange about Mr. Logan."

A chair clatters to the ground. "Professor?" the woman calls out.

More voices. Footsteps. People leaving. Confusion.

I can't pay attention. Something is happening to my hands. To my knuckles. Something strange. *They hurt.* These aren't pinches anymore. This is real pain. And it's getting worse.

One part of my brain registers a person entering the room. A technician.

"Professor!" he calls on the intercom. "There's something happening to Mr. Logan's hands!"

I hear static. Must be his orders coming through. "Yes, sir," the technician says. "Okay, sir." Then he comes up close to my tank.

What are they going to do now? I'm in so much pain! I can't think straight! It's too much. I've got to stop this.

I leap from the tank.

The next thing I know, the technician is on the floor. There's blood everywhere. I look down at my throbbing hands. But they're not just hands anymore. They're claws. Bloody claws!

A door opens. People rush to the glass wall.

"Over here, Professor," someone calls out. "Behind the glass! The tech is dead! Logan has...he's killed him!"

There is silence. Then a chuckle. It's the man they call the Professor.

"We must operate again," he says. "Now we must control his mind. Logan is a mutant with extraordinary healing powers. And when we're finished, his skeleton, his claws, and his powers will be ours!" I can see him smile.

I'm in a fog. Nothing makes sense. But I know what the Professor is: an enemy. My body reacts. I break through the glass wall that separates me from him. I feel no remorse. I see only my enemy. And I'm filled with hate. Hate for what I've become.

I go for the Professor, vaulting through the air. Closer...closer...then there's a ripping sound.

The tubes fall from my body. I've pulled them too far. My life support is giving way. Everything is fading.

CHAPTER 7

Weapon X/ Phase 3: The Controls

Trees. Snow. Sky. The nightmare continues. I'm outside, in the woods. Naked. But I don't feel cold. I don't feel much of anything.

I've got a helmet on my head. But it's not for protection. I'm getting signals through it. A battery pack is slung around my waist.

The signals tell me when to move, what to do. I'm being controlled. But they can't control all of me. I know I am still a human.

I sniff the air and smell an enemy. There's a kind of scent to it. I zero in on a video camera hidden in some foliage. I'm being watched. But I feel something else out there. And it's coming closer. All my senses come alive.

Snikt! My claws come out. My heart beats faster. Then, out of nowhere, a grizzly bear appears.

I don't think. I receive the signal: *fight for your life!* Seconds later, the grizzly is on the ground. And I'm standing—victorious—in a pool of its blood.

I hear a click. The video camera shuts off. Suddenly I feel odd. The signals are getting fainter. Somebody is turning me off! I feel helpless. I can barely keep my eyes open.

But something inside me is still awake.

Guards come. They lead me back inside the compound. But when I see the Professor, something snaps and I'm strong again. I receive the signal to strike. One by one, the guards fall to the floor.

The Professor backs away. "I turned you off, beast," he shouts. "I shut you down! *I order you* to turn...yourself...off!" I keep coming at the Professor. "I need help here! Somebody... what's happening here?" screams the Professor.

I hate the Professor, and part of me wants to see him dead. But I'm not acting on my own. Someone is controlling me. Someone *other* than the Professor.

More guards arrive. I kill all of them. But the Professor has escaped!

Hunt him down, the signal tells me. *Hunt him down!*

I pick up his scent and track him through the compound. I can smell that I'm closing in on him.

Quietly, I pad into a huge chamber. Past signs that read DANGER: ADAMANTIUM REACTOR. It's hot here. Very hot.

The giant cone-shaped room looks like the inside of a rocket ship. Everywhere, metal gleams brightly. I'm standing at a railing that runs around the middle of the cone.

At the top, there's a spout coming out of the dome. It's spewing balls of chemical fire.

At the bottom, there's a woman lying on

the floor. Has she fallen? Slowly she gets up. She screams. I recognize her—she's from the Weapon X team.

I get the signal to *hunt*. *Hurt*. I leap into the pit beside her. The heat is building.

"Mr. Logan," she says. "Please, please, don't hurt me."

Somehow I find the words. My own words—not given to me by any signal.

I say, "I don't...want...to hurt you."

Suddenly the ceiling dome opens wide. More spouts. More bursts of flame.

"The Professor threw me into the pit to trap you," the woman is saying. "And now he's going to blow up the reactor! Run, Mr. Logan. Run!"

The Professor's laugh echoes through the chamber. Flames shoot down. I'm hit again and again. I'm on fire!

"I'll destroy you like you tried to destroy me," the Professor shouts. "I am in control here!"

But the air suddenly cools down. Somebody has turned the reactor off. Somebody else is controlling it! My healing factor begins to kick in.

I climb a ladder to the control booth. The Professor doesn't notice. He's busy trying to work the controls. It's useless.

There's only a window between us now. I break through it.

"You...you're...you're...*dead!*" the Professor stutters.

I grab him tightly. "Am I...dead?" I say. "Is...that what...you've...done to me?...Made me a walking...*dead man?*"

"You're an animal," the Professor spits out. "A trained animal."

"*I...am...Logan!*" I say. "I...am...a man. You...are the...animal!"

And I toss him into the reactor.

As his cries fade away, so do the control booth, the reactor, the compound...

CHAPTER 8

....

Weapon X/
Phase 4:
The Setup

A desk, a bed, a lamp. Slowly, things come into focus. I'm in my bedroom in the X-Men's mansion. And somebody is calling my name.

"Hey, Wolvie! Wolvie!" It's Jubilee.

I'm not sure why, but I have a real soft spot for Jubilee. She's a kid. Kind of a pain in the neck, really. She hasn't been an X-Man very long, and she likes hanging around me, so I let her. Sometimes. I open the window and poke my head out.

"Come on out!" she calls from the basket-ball court. Beast, Rogue, Gambit, and Cyclops are there too.

"These guys won't let me play without you," she says. "We can be a team!"

"I'm not much of a team player, darlin'. Especially not in my free time," I say. "Catch you later." And I close the window.

I turn my back on Jubilee, the X-Men, and the game.

Exhausted, I rub my eyes. And when I open them, I'm somewhere else.

The place is familiar. It's the Weapon X compound. But I can't remember what has happened to me. My helmet and battery pack are gone. Bodies lie on the floor around me. Guards. They've been killed. And my hands are covered with blood! Suddenly everything comes rushing back. The pain. The claws. I did it. I killed the guards. Me. Logan.

I stagger outside, into the snow. "You're still Logan," I tell myself. "You're still a man."

But I know that's not true.

I rip through the compound fence to escape. But I can't escape what I've become.

I haven't gotten far when suddenly I'm face-to-face with a Siberian tiger. For a second, I just stand there, wondering what a tiger is doing in Canada. I'm not receiving any signals. Nobody is telling me what to do.

Then instinct kicks in. I leap at the tiger with my claws out. It almost makes me laugh

out loud! The tiger is deadly. But so am I!

The cat is soon lying lifeless in the snow.

My instinct tells me something else. I'm being watched. Again.

But who? I killed all the guards. And the Professor. But I can smell a human scent. I track it.

There's a group of guards, standing in a clearing. The same guards I just saw dead!

They lift their guns and take aim at me.

In a split second, everything comes together. The reactor, the deaths—it was a set-up. They want me to *think* I'm an animal. A beast.

Before they can shoot, I attack. Wouldn't want to disappoint anyone. This time they won't get back up.

A security alarm goes off as I make my way back into the compound. I move low, sniffing the air for my prey.

I stop before a steel door. He's inside. I'd know his scent anywhere.

Snikt! Out come the claws. Down comes the door.

The Professor is too scared to speak. There's nowhere for him to run.

Quietly, I circle him. He's frozen to the spot—like a deer caught in headlights. *He's* the animal, I tell myself. *Not* me.

And then I remember his frightened cries. "I shut you down! *Turn…yourself…off!*"

My claws are inches from his face. I'm about to strike. But I stop. Somebody *else* is controlling me. Not the Professor. He didn't even know I was a mutant. He was surprised. But the person who did know…the person who knew my adamantium claws and my new skeleton would make me unstoppable…that person is my enemy. The Professor is nothing.

I retract my claws, leaving the Professor and the Weapon X compound behind.

I head out into the snow, and the glaring white of the wilderness becomes the glaring light of an overhead bulb.

CHAPTER 9

....

The Hulk

Maps. Flags. Uniforms. I'm in army headquarters.

"We're ready to mobilize," a captain is saying to me. He points to a screen. A blip is moving across it.

"The Hulk is back in Canada," the captain continues. "We must stop him. Official orders. And as our number one government agent..."

The captain puts his hand on my shoulder. Quickly, I jerk away. Yeah, I work for the government. And yeah, I've taken a code name: Wolverine. And for the most part, I even follow orders. But I'm not going to stand for this buddy-buddy stuff.

The captain pretends not to notice.

"Your assignment," he says sternly, "is to bring down the Hulk."

The Hulk, huh? I'd heard of him. The seven-foot, thousand-pound alter ego of Doctor Bruce Banner is supposed to be the most powerful creature on earth. Seems Banner received a megadose of gamma radiation at some nuclear bomb testing site, and now, when he gets stressed out, he transforms into a mean green destruction machine.

Well, I have something of a destructive side myself. The government is aware of it. They know I'm a mutant with special powers. They know about my adamantium skeleton, too. That's why they hired me. Guess they think it's time they got their money's worth.

An hour later I'm being air-dropped into the remote north woods. Nice place. Nothing out here but trees and wild animals. I should fit in perfectly. I start my search.

For five hours I wander through the woods, looking for tracks. Startling squirrels.

Finally, my super-sharp hearing homes in on some heavy thuds and grunts, like two big office buildings jumping up and down. Hmmm. Maybe the Hulk isn't traveling alone? But I don't have time to ponder the possibilities. I've only got one more hour to do my job.

I burst into a clearing. There's the Hulk, all right, squaring off with some white behemoth. It doesn't matter. I can take on them both.

"All right, you freaks," I snarl. "Just hold it. If you really want to tangle with someone, try me."

I hurl myself between them, breaking up the fight. "Heads up, tough guys," I say. "The Wolverine is coming through."

The Hulk is confused. He doesn't strike me as especially bright.

"Huh?" he says. "Little man attacks Hulk?"

"That's about the size of it, sonny," I say, leaping onto his back.

The Hulk spins around. "Stand still," he tells me. "Or Hulk will smash!"

The Hulk is two feet taller than me. And he's five times as heavy as me. I'm not about to stop moving. No way.

"Nope," I say. "Moving's what I do best."

I jump over his head like we're playing leapfrog and land near the other monster—the furry one. So far, he's just been hanging around, watching. Well, that's going to change!

Skrat! The beast is surprised by the attack. He stumbles back. I press on, giving a hefty kick to his stomach. *Choom!* The beast goes flying. And as he does, he cries out one word: "Wen-di-go!"

So that's Wendigo?

I've heard of him before, but I thought he was just a legend—like Sasquatch. Wendigo: The legendary eight-foot shaggy monster of the great North. Supposed to be immortal. Yeah, right!

In an instant, Wendigo leaps back up. Well, maybe there's *something* to that legend.

I turn to face the Hulk. He's watching me fight Wendigo, and looking pretty bewildered. "First little man fights Hulk," he says. "And now he fights Hulk's enemy?" A light bulb goes on over his dim little head. "Then little man must be Hulk's friend. Yes! Hulk's friend. Hulk will help little man fight Hulk's enemy."

Wendigo comes at me. But the Hulk jumps to my defense. The big green brute thinks I'm his buddy—this is a misconception I can make use of!

"Hulk and Hulk's friend will smash Wendigo!" the Hulk roars.

"Okay, my friend," I say, jumping onto Wendigo's back. "Quickly! While I've got him distracted. Attack!"

I do the leapfrog move again. In a flash, the Hulk spins Wendigo high in the air and tosses him into a group of trees. *Kroom!* The trees crack with the force.

I can't believe it! The shaggy beast is still conscious. The Hulk did his best. But it just wasn't good enough. It's up to me to finish this little skirmish. And fast.

Snikt! I hurl myself against Wendigo. We both go down. Only I get back up. The beast is down for the count.

"Ha!" the Hulk cries out. "Little man did good. Wendigo dead."

"No, Hulk," I answer, brushing myself off. "He should be, but he's only unconscious. Seems like he really is immortal."

For a moment, we stand there in silence. The Hulk peers at me. He's curious, wondering who I am. Well, I'll end the suspense.

"All right, greenskin," I say, giving him an all-out punch. "It's your turn to take a thrashing!"

The Hulk barely flinches. "Huh?" he says. Then an angry light comes into his eyes. "You betrayed Hulk. Just like all puny humans!"

Uh-oh. The green guy is seeing red. Time to move. I bob and weave. He's having a tough time catching me. But I'm having a tougher time doing any damage to him. I slash out with my claws. But the dim-witted monster won't go down! And I'm losing steam. How long can I hold out?

The Hulk lifts a giant boulder like it's a marshmallow. He's just about to pancake me with it when we hear the putt-putt sound of a helicopter. The Hulk drops the rock in surprise. And we both freeze in mid-step. The 'copter says RCAF on the side. Royal Canadian Air Force.

"Attention, Wolverine," a voice booms out from a bullhorn. "Your six hours are over. You have failed. It is now our turn."

Failed? I wasn't down yet!

"No way!" I shout back. "You can't do this to me. I've just gotten started!"

The voice gets louder. "You have your

orders, Wolverine. Do not disobey. Enter the lift capsule now."

They lower a capsule. "But what about the Hulk?" I ask.

"We will take care of the Hulk" is their answer.

I'm not happy about it, but I board the capsule.

They drop a sleeping gas bomb, and in a few moments, the Hulk's out cold. Poor moron. He never knew what hit him.

I spot Wendigo sleeping like a baby, hidden behind some trees. I've got to laugh. Should I tell these guys about him? Nah. They want me to follow orders? I'll follow orders. But they never said anything about any Wendigo.

Four air force guys attach a rope to the Hulk and drag him into a steel cage. They connect the cage to the helicopter and we take off.

From inside I can look down at the Hulk. He's beginning to stir. Nothing can keep him out for long.

"Cage?" he says, looking all around. "Puny humans think they can keep Hulk prisoner? Puny humans wrong!"

He swings his arms wildly. The steel bars break apart. Then he steps out of the cage and into the air, tumbling to the ground.

"We lost him!" somebody cries. "We lost the Hulk!"

The helicopter hovers for a moment. But the Hulk is already dusting himself off and lumbering out of sight.

Yeah, I think. They lost the Hulk. Most entertaining thing I've seen in some time. You've got to give the old Hulkster credit. He doesn't let himself be pushed around by any "puny humans"!

Unlike me. I'm always being pushed around. Go on this mission, Wolverine. Do this, Wolverine. Don't do that, Wolverine. I'm like a dog on a leash—not a wolverine.

If only I could act when and how I want to act. Who knows? Maybe someday.

All at once, the sky outside the window disappears. Instead of clouds, I'm passing...

CHAPTER 10

Professor Xavier

Jeeps. Trucks. Road signs. I'm whizzing by them on my motorcycle. Minutes later I race through a high-security gate. I'm at the headquarters of a top-secret government agency.

A guard shakes his fist at me. As usual, I didn't stop for clearance.

I just laugh. Sure, this is a top-secret agency. But I'm their *top* secret agent. And in my Wolverine uniform, hey, who did he *think* I was, Tinker Bell?

I park in a space labeled RESERVED.

"Reserved" means reserved for generals or agency directors, I know. "But not today," I say out loud. "I have a meeting!"

Honestly, though, I'm in no rush. I hate meetings. And I don't even know what this little confab is about. I understand somebody important wants to meet me. Big deal. What do they want, my autograph? I take my sweet time getting there.

At last I saunter into an office. "They're waiting for you in the conference room, sir," a secretary says, trying to hurry me along.

"Let them wait" is my answer. "It's good for the soul."

I push open the door. "All right, gents. I'm here. Now, who's this bigwig you want me to meet?"

"I'm the bigwig," says a bald man in a wheelchair. "My name is Professor Charles Xavier." He wheels around to face me.

"I'm supposed to be impressed?"

That's when the commanding officer steps in.

"The top brass is impressed," he says. "And

the Professor is here to make you an offer."

I remember something about another professor. An evil one. But the memory is fuzzy. It doesn't stick. Besides, I like *this* professor right away. Something in his eyes tells me he's different, like me. A mutant. Plus I'm curious about the offer. I lean closer.

"I'll come straight to the point," Professor Xavier says. "I know about your battle with the Hulk. More important, I know about your powers. I have a need for mutants. A desperate need."

Mutants, huh? This is getting interesting.

"But what about my position here?" I ask, playing it cool.

"I'm offering you a chance to become a free agent," Professor Xavier tells me. "You can learn to use your powers for the greatest good."

Hmmm. I'm not against the greatest good. In fact, I'm all for it. And the way I see it, the greatest good for me would be to get out of this dead-end job. Escape all the red tape. I wouldn't have to follow another government order—or see another security guard. Ever!

It doesn't take me long to decide.

"Okay, Professor," I say. "You've found your man."

"What?" the CO exclaims. Why is he so surprised? I never pretended to be happy here.

"Not so fast, fella," he says. "The Canadian

government has put a lot of time and money into training you. Just try walking out on us and I'll have you locked up so fast, you won't know what hit you!"

I shake my head sadly—the way a disappointed teacher shakes his head at a slow student. *Snikt!* I let loose one lone claw and point it at him, like I'm going to lecture.

"It seems you don't get my meaning, friend." My voice is so low it's a growl.

I take a step toward the CO. He takes a step back.

"This is still a free country, isn't it? I'm resigning my commission."

R-i-i-i-p! Like a flash of lightning, I slice the CO's tie in half.

"Effective immediately!"

I bring my claw close to his chin. "Do you have any objections?" I ask.

He shakes his head no.

"I didn't think you would," I say, retracting my claw.

I turn to leave. The Professor is at my side. But the CO has found his tongue.

"Believe me, mister," he calls after us. "You haven't heard the last of this."

Yeah. He's big talk now—now that I'm halfway out the door.

"Anytime you want me, bub," I tell him, "you know where to look. Come on, Prof. Let's go."

And just like that, I'm starting a new life.

A new life!

Then the flashback is over, and I'm awake. It all seemed so simple back then. Now I know nothing is that simple. Even what you don't know can come back to haunt you.

I look out my window again. The X-Men— all except Jubilee—are shooting hoops. They seem so happy. Nothing tugging at *their* memories. We're all mutants. But I still feel different. And I felt that way from the first time I met them. One memory stands out in my mind. Maybe it will help me understand.

Let's see. I had just become an X-Man when it happened. "Concentrate," I tell myself. "Concentrate on the past."

And suddenly I'm back in another time.

CHAPTER 11

•••••••••••••••••••••••

Jean

Clouds. Blue sky. A gleaming control panel. I'm sitting on board the X-Men's stratojet. The Blackbird.

All the X-Men are here too. And I do mean *all* the X-Men. The new X-Men—me included—have just wrapped up our first assignment: to rescue the old X-Men from the island-sized mutant, Krakoa.

Well, we did it. Everyone's safe and sound. And now we're heading back to the mansion in Westchester County. My new home. My new *home?*

The place is gonna be crowded. Well,

crowded for me. I count heads. Thirteen mutants. Thirteen wild cards. And I could be the wildest card of all. What have I gotten myself into? I hate group activities.

You've got to relax, I tell myself. You're going to be living with these guys. Give them a chance.

I wouldn't mind giving the redhead sitting in front of me a chance. I have a special sense about her—even though we haven't said more than two words to each other. She's one of the old X-Men, the ones who were trapped on Krakoa. When it came time to be rescued, Cyclops got to carry her out. Lucky one-eyed mutant.

I watch Jean—that's her name, Jean Grey—lean forward and whisper something to Cyclops. He smiles, and they both laugh. Are these two an item, or what? We begin our descent. I spot the mansion below. "Be it ever so humble..." I say to Banshee with a big fake grin on my puss.

"Ah yes, me lad! 'Tis good to be home!" he says in this thick Irish brogue that makes me realize I'm *never* going to fit in with these people.

Fit in or not, it *will* feel good to plant my feet on solid ground again. After that Krakoa business, I wouldn't mind feeling some dirt between my toes that isn't going to suck the life out of me. The jet does a vertical landing, then glides into its hangar. What do you know? We're here.

Everyone crowds the exit. "This might be a problem," says Havok, Cyclops' brother. I can tell he isn't talking about safety regulations, either. He's talking about having thirteen X-Men around in one place.

"What's Charles going to do with all of us?" he asks as everyone files out.

The Professor is waiting for us on the airstrip. "Welcome back," he says. "Each one of you did excellent work."

We make phony small talk among ourselves. But what each of us is really thinking about is that there are too many X-Men. Who's going to stay on the team? And who's going to leave? Me, I'm here for the long haul.

I don't like taking orders from anybody—especially not this Cyclops character—but being an X-Man beats being in the army.

"Thanks to you," says the Professor, "Krakoa has vanished off the face of the earth."

"Yeah," says the winged mutant called Angel. "Good thing the Hulk wasn't there. Then we'd have been in real trouble." He chuckles like this is hysterical. I don't find it very funny.

That's the second crack he's made about my battle with the Hulk. My eyes narrow. The Hulk is still a sore spot. I step close to Angel and—*snikt!*—gently brush a claw against his wing.

"You should know something about me," I say. "I don't like being the butt of your jokes."

Cyclops steps between us. "Calm down, Wolverine," he says. "Angel was just trying to be funny."

"Yes, Wolverine," the Professor adds. "We've got to work *with* each other. Not *against* each other."

He sounds angry. But hey, I'm angry too.

I'm just as tough as any of the X-Men here.
And I'd be happy to prove it.

I remind myself I've got to give these
mutants a chance. Do I want to return to intel-
ligence work? Taking orders from a bunch of
pasty-faced, stab-you-in-the-back good old
boys? No thanks. I can deal with this. I retract
my claw and give a shrug. Then I storm off.

Alone.

I walk around the mansion. The grounds here are pretty nice. Wooded in places, with a lot of gardens, and lawns, too. "This is nice, but it ain't no Wood Buffalo National Park," I'm thinking, when I notice somebody up ahead. Somebody with red hair. Jean.

"Hey, wait up!" I call out as I catch up to her.

She smiles at me. "I'm glad to see you, Wolverine," she says, brushing some of that red hair out of her eyes. Man, is she something. "I wanted to tell you before that I thought Angel was out of line."

We keep walking, and Jean tells me about herself, about her telekinetic powers. How they make some things really easy, and others really difficult. "Sometimes I wish I led a normal life," she says, "that I wasn't a mutant." She looks me in the eyes. "I guess we always want what we can't have."

"I knew what I wanted the minute I laid eyes on you," I say, leaning close. "And what Wolverine wants, he gets."

"You might not know this," she says to me. "Scott—you know, Cyclops—and I are a couple."

But she doesn't move away from me. I can feel the electricity between us.

Then, out of nowhere, Angel shows up.

"You heard the lady, shrimp," he shouts, landing practically on top of me. "Back off. Jean is Scott's girlfriend. And even if she weren't, she's too good for the likes of you!"

What's with this guy? Either he really doesn't like me, or he really likes Jean. The only thing I know for sure is that I'm *really* mad.

"Too good for me? I think you're confused, pal," I snarl. "That's for the lady to decide, not *you*." My claws slice through the air, through feathers, through everything around me. But Angel is too fast for me to make much contact.

Jean is crying out for us to stop when a lightning bolt flashes between Angel and me. We draw back. Storm is standing next to Jean, and she doesn't look happy.

"Remember the Professor's words," she says staring me straight in the eye. Then she turns and strides away.

"That little guy's crazy!" says Angel, hurrying to catch up to her. "He tried to get me with those claws. How could the Professor have brought a lunatic like that into the mansion?"

Storm says something I can't make out and their voices fade away.

I expect Jean to leave also. But she doesn't.

"I'm not afraid of you," she says. "I feel your pain."

I can't even look at her. I feel too ashamed. How could I attack an X-Man like that? I went berserk!

"Flyboy's right," I say to Jean. "I really am bad news. As crazy as they come."

Before she can say anything else, I turn around and walk away. I'm better off being alone. But behind me is a different place. I've stepped back into the present. Into my bedroom in the mansion.

Better off alone? I can't believe that now. I shut my eyes and try to think of something, *anything* to make me remember otherwise.

CHAPTER 12

●●●●●●●●●●●●●●●●●●●●●●●●●

The X-Men

Well-kept lawns. Trimmed hedges. Flower gardens. I'm still walking the grounds of the X-Men's mansion. But it's a different time. Later.

Of course, I'm alone. The rest of the team is probably hanging out together somewhere enjoying themselves. When I first joined the group, they used to ask me to come too. Even after my blow-up with Angel, they kept trying to include me.

"We're going out for pizza," Cyclops, the leader of the team, would say. "Want to come along?"

Or "It's bowling night." Or "How about

going to the movies?"

I said no for a long time. Now when I'm beginning to think pizza, or bowling, or a movie would be fun—no one's asking. Oh well. So I'm not buddy-buddy with the X-Men. I'm used to being alone anyway.

Then Professor X calls me.

"Logan, please come see me," he says. Only he isn't anywhere nearby saying this. His voice is in my head. He's sending me a tele-pathic, or mental, message.

"I'm on my way," I think back to him. And by the time I finish my thought, I'm knocking at his door.

"Come in, Logan," the Professor says as he waves me into a chair. We're both facing a big TV screen. He pushes a button, and a newscast comes on.

"Please watch this," he says.

A reporter stands in front of a burning building. "Witnesses claim this fire is the work of a mutant," the reporter is saying. "A quick-moving, animal-like mutant. No one saw the creature clearly. But it is said to have claws.

And it left behind this—a glove."

I'm dumbstruck for a moment. "That's my glove!" I say. "What's going on?"

"Please keep watching," the Professor says. He switches channels.

Another reporter is standing on a street corner in the midst of a riot. Cars are overturned. Store windows are smashed. Sirens are screaming. And the reporter is holding up a mask. *My* mask!

"This item was found on the scene," the reporter says. "It is said to belong to a mutant called Wolverine, a member of the X-Men. The X-Men were formed to bring humans and mutants together in peace. But they seem to be doing just the opposite. Police are hoping to bring Wolverine in by nightfall."

Professor X pushes the button again, and the screen goes blank.

"I've been here all day!" I shout. "It couldn't have been me!"

"I know, Logan. I know," the Professor answers. "Of course it wasn't you. But that mutant—or whoever it was—wants people to *think* it was you. You must be very careful now. Don't leave the mansion. And please stay close to the other X-Men. Now, if you'll excuse me, I have a lot of thinking to do."

"Yeah, me too," I mumble as I leave the Professor's office. "Someone's setting me up for a fall. But who?"

I check my closet. Natch—one of my spare uniforms is missing. But how could anyone get into my room? He or she would be picked up by Cerebro's security system as soon as they got anywhere *near* the mansion. And that computer never slips up!

Unless...it was someone already in the mansion.

I shake the thought from my head. "No," I say. "That's crazy!"

Still, I know I can't trust anyone. I've learned that by now.

All at once, the mansion feels like a prison. I've got to get outside. I have to think.

I reach for my jacket. There's a note in the pocket!

"Meet me at the top of the Empire State

Building at midnight."

Of course it's not signed. And it's typed, too, so I can't tell anything by the handwriting. But I know it's from him. The guy who wants to bring me down. I rush outside.

"Hey, Logan! Where are you going?" Cyclops waves to me from across the lawn.

Trust no one.

"Oh, just getting some fresh air," I say.

A second later, I'm tearing up the road on my motorcycle. Destination: New York City.

Nobody gives me a second glance. Of course I'm not in uniform. But I've got my Wolverine suit on under my street clothes. When I meet this dirtbag, I want everything to be official.

I check my watch. The observation deck will close pretty soon. And I have an appointment to keep.

At the Empire State Building I pay for my ticket like anyone else. I take the elevator up to the top.

Not much of a crowd this late at night. The place is almost empty. I can easily survey the layout. A high wall—kind of like a guard rail—circles the deck. There are those binocular-type machines too. The kind you put money in to look at Jersey. They look like giant parking meters.

I walk around a bit. The view *is* pretty spectacular. A guard is making his final rounds. The souvenir shop closes. One by one, people are filing into the elevator.

As quietly as I can, I sneak into a dark corner. The guard walks right by. He doesn't notice a thing.

Finally I'm alone. At least I think I am. I step out from the dark in my Wolverine costume.

Somebody grabs me from behind with one hand. The other yanks my arms back in a superstrong grip.

"Glad you could make it on such short notice," a voice growls in my ear. I recognize it right away. Sabretooth! My old enemy. I should have known. Animal-like. Claws. Mutant. No wonder people were confused.

There's another reason, too. Sabretooth

has always had it in for me. Although I don't know why.

"So tell me, catbreath," I say. "How did you steal my glove and mask?"

"It was easy!" he says with a laugh. "Remember that rash of mutant crime a few weeks ago?

"Well," he continues, "I knew that Cerebro would be busy tracking Magneto, Mastermind, and all the major mutant menaces. The crime wave was so bad, in fact, it occurred to me Cerebro might even be overloaded. So I waited outside the mansion. Then, when all the X-Men were out being heroes, I scaled the walls. I was barely a blip on its screen. Don't forget, Wolverine. My tread can be feather-light. Or rock-hard."

As he says that, Sabretooth kicks me. *Oof!* I'm thrown clear across the deck.

"I've got your costume, Wolverine. And now I'm going to get you!"

"Not if I can help it," I say. *Snikt!*

We exchange punches. Blow for blow, we're evenly matched. But then Sabretooth strikes out with such incredible force that my head snaps back—and hits one of the giant binoculars. For a few seconds, I'm out cold.

But that's long enough for Sabretooth to grab my hands and swing me over the guard rail. When I come to, I'm dangling off the roof of the Empire State Building!

"Leave the X-Men, Wolverine," Sabretooth says. "Join me. Together, nothing can stop us."

Those words! I remember someone else saying them. Someone with blond hair. A crew cut. I see him for an instant—superimposed over Sabretooth. And then it's gone. All I see is Sabretooth. My enemy.

"Join me," he says again, "and I'll let you live."

"Never!" I spit at him. I don't care if I die. How could I have thought the X-Men—*my friends!*—set me up?

Suddenly, a force beam blasts Sabretooth, and he drops me. I'm hurtling down. One floor. Two floors. Three floors. I'm picking up speed. Floor after floor zooms past. It occurs to me that I *am* going to die.

All at once, gentle gloved hands scoop me up in midfall. "Y'all better ease up on those rich desserts, Wolvie," says Rogue. "Ah can hardly wrap my arms around you!"

I can barely believe it. "Rogue," I say weakly. "Thanks."

"Don't mention it, shugah," she says. "We're all here. Cyclops found that note you dropped on your bedroom floor. He, Beast, Gambit, and Jean are on the roof right now, playing tag with your pussycat friend."

When Sabretooth sees me—alive and well and in a *really* bad mood by now—he leaps into the air and over the wall. Jean and Rogue take off after him. But I know he's gone. The cat's a master hunter. And he knows the flip side of the coin, too. It's all part of the chase.

Sabretooth has disappeared. And now the Empire State Building is growing dim, too. The memory is over. But one thing is clear. My friendship with the X-Men.

The Present: The Mansion

"*Tres bien* shot!" Gambit calls out. The X-Men are *still* playing basketball. Laughing. Carrying on. Having fun. Something *I* should have more often, I think. Fun. With my friends.

So my past is a mystery. I know I've got unfinished business with Silver Fox. Creed. Sabretooth. But for now? Now it's time to shoot some hoops.

I take one more glance in the mirror. "So, bub," I say out loud. "What are you waiting for? Move those chops."

I race downstairs, then outside. Maybe someday my dreams...flashbacks...whatever... will make sense.

But in the meantime...

I think little Jubilee needs a teammate.

If you liked this book, here's a taste of...

Second Genesis

"Huh?" Cyclops stood there stunned, uncomprehending. He had thought they would be overjoyed to be rescued, happy that he had come back for them. He certainly hadn't expected this!

"You fool!" Angel shouted. "Don't you understand? It wanted you to come back—and bring others with you! It was all a trap—and now it's too late!"

Cyclops stared around him at the ruins of the collapsed building. Even as he watched, the earth seemed to slowly swallow the remaining rubble. And now, the horrifying truth was beginning to dawn upon him. Now, when it was indeed, as Angel had said, too late...

BOOKS IN THIS SERIES

Days of Future Past

Second Genesis

Wolverine: Top Secret

The Xavier Files